SCHOOL!

ADVENTURES AT THE
HARVEY N. TROUBLE
ELEMENTARY SCHOOL

Gladys Friday

Cutie Pie

Iona Tricycle

Janitor Iquit
Assistant Janitor Quitoo

Ms. Celia Seeyalater

Abby Birthday

Ms. Roxanne Pebbles

Mr. Norman Don't-know

Mrs. Doremi Fasollatido

Ron Faster

Chuckie Upkins

Mr. Hugh da Mann

Anita Dawg

Moose

SCHOOL!

ADVENTURES AT THE
HARVEY N. TROUBLE
ELEMENTARY SCHOOL

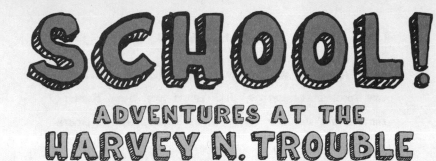

Written by Kate McMullan

Inspired and Illustrated by George Booth

SQUARE FISH   FEIWEL AND FRIENDS · NEW YORK

ACKNOWLEDGMENTS

MANY THANKS TO MY YOWIE-KA-ZOWIE AGENT, HOLLY MCGHEE;

MY SUPER-DUPER EDITORS, JEAN FEIWEL AND MARIA BARBO;

AND THE ONE AND ONLY, HOTSY-TOTSY GENIUS, GEORGE BOOTH

—K. M.

SQUARE
FISH

An Imprint of Macmillan

Library of Congress Cataloging-in-Publication Data
McMullan, Kate.
School! : adventures at the Harvey N. Trouble Elementary School / written by Kate McMullan ;
inspired and illustrated by George Booth.
p.   cm.
Audience: "AR: 3.9 / LEXILE: 660L."
Summary: Chronicles a week in the life of Ron Faster, whose famous parents are both
seeking work, whose bus driver, Mr. Stuckinaditch, keeps making him late, and who
must adjust to substitute teacher Mr. Don't-know while Mrs. Petzgalore is away.
ISBN 978-0-312-55595-5
[1. Schools—Fiction.   2. Family life—Fiction.   3. Humorous stories.]
I. Booth, George, 1926- ill.   II. Title.
PZ7.M47879Scd 2012   [Fic]—dc23   2012007637

Originally published in the United States by Feiwel and Friends
First Square Fish Edition: July 2012
Square Fish logo designed by Filomena Tuosto
Story idea by George Booth
Book design by Barbara Grzeslo
mackids.com

2 4 6 8 10 9 7 5 3

AR: 3.9 / LEXILE: 660L

For my Price School pals, Gayle and Marky
—K. M.

For Dad, William E. Booth,

Missouri superintendent of schools, 43 years;

and Mother, Norene Booth,

who taught grades one through eight
—G. B.

SCHOOL!

ADVENTURES AT THE
HARVEY N. TROUBLE
ELEMENTARY SCHOOL

Contents

CHAPTER 1

HOTSY-TOTSY MONDAY

On Monday morning, Ron Faster

ran downstairs—*fast.*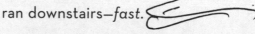

He found his parents sitting at the kitchen

table, reading the Help Wanted ads in the newspaper.

Ron's father, Mr. Hugo Faster, looked up from his paper. "Good

morning, son," he said.

"I've made you a batch of Wavey Waffles, Ron, dear,"

said Ron's mother, Mrs. Cookie Faster.

Ron slid into a chair and helped himself to a waffle.

Its top looked like waves breaking on the seashore.

He poured on some Surf's Up Syrup and dug in.

"Yum, Mom," said Ron, taking a second waffle.

"Any jobs for you in the paper today?"

"Not a one," said Mrs. Faster. "There are lots

of jobs for fast-food cooks," she added. "But just because I

cook fast doesn't mean I cook

fast food."

Ron

"Any jobs for you, Dad?" asked Ron.

Mr. Faster shook his head. "Nope," he said. "Not a single

job for a retired race car driver. You'd better be off, son," he added.

"You don't want to miss the school bus."

"Don't worry," said Ron. "I won't."

Ron finished his waffles. He kissed his mother and he kissed

his father, and he ran out of his big, old, full-of-junk,

tumbledown house, down the front porch steps and up

the dirt road—*fast.*

He ran past the garden, where his mother grew all

sorts of strange and mysterious

plants.

He ran past the barn, where his father kept his old green race car.

He ran all the way to the bus stop. Half a minute later, the school bus driver, Mr. Ivan Stuckinaditch, stopped to pick him up.

"Good morning, Mr. Stuckinaditch," said Ron Faster as he boarded the bus. "Are you going to get stuck in a ditch today?"

"Why would I do that?" asked Mr. Stuckinaditch.

Mr. Stuckinaditch drove to the next stop and picked up Viola Fuss. Then he picked up little Izzy Normal.

Viola Fuss

Izzy Normal

He picked up all the kids and was driving them to school when all of a sudden . . . **CLONK!**

The front of the bus bounced up in the air.

"Zowie!" cried Viola Fuss. "What's going on?"

This is Not NORMAL, said little Izzy Normal.

"What's wrong, Mr. Stuckinaditch?" called Ron Faster.

"I believe we have run into a problem," said Mr. Stuckinaditch.

He pressed on the gas pedal:

Vrrrrm! Vrrrrm!

The bus didn't move.

"Are we stuck in a ditch, Mr. Stuckinaditch?" asked Viola Fuss.

"Maybe that's the problem," said Mr. Stuckinaditch.

"I'll go get help," said Ron. He jumped off the bus and took off running—*fast*.

Soon, Ron ran back—*fast*. Right behind him came Mr. Justin Case, driving a sky-blue tow truck.

Mr. Justin Case got out of his tow truck and examined the problem.

"You're stuck in a ditch," he said.

"That's right," said Mr. Stuckinaditch. "Nice to meet you."

"Lucky for you, I always carry a chain—just in case," said Mr. Justin Case.

He hooked one end of the chain to the front bumper of the school bus, and the other end to his tow truck. He climbed back into his tow truck, and pulled the bus out of the ditch.

All the bus riders cheered, Mr. Justin Case unhooked his chain. Mr. Stuckinaditch thanked him. Then, Mr. Justin Case drove off in his sky-blue tow truck, and Mr. Stuckinaditch drove the kids to school.

The kids jumped off the bus and there was the principal,

7

Miss Ingashoe, walking around the parking lot.

"This is not normal," said little Izzy Normal.

"What's wrong, Miss Ingashoe?" Ron asked her.

"I am missing something," said the principal.

"What?" asked Viola Fuss.

"Never you mind," said Miss Ingashoe.

"I'll find it sooner or later. Have a hotsy-totsy Monday!"

Miss Ingashoe walked off then, which was not so easy, because

she was missing something.

The kids ran past the playground,

where the science teacher's dog, Einstein,

was digging a hole, and into the

Harvey N. Trouble School.

Janitor Iquit was

standing inside the door, mopping something up.

"Watch yer step," said Assistant Janitor Quitoo. "Watch yer step."

One of the kindergartners wrinkled her nose. WHAT SMELLS? she asked.

"How should I know?" said Chuckie Upkins passing by,

heading in the direction of the nurse's office. Nurse's Office →

Ron and his friends watched their steps going through the

reception area as Oopsie Spiller appeared, carrying a plastic cup.

"Look!" said Oopsie. "I'm bringing my teacher a glass of orange—

OOPS!"

The cup flew out of Oopsie's hand. Orange

juice splattered everywhere.

The janitors stared at the juice all over the floor.

"I have an important announcement," said Janitor Iquit.

"What is it?" asked Assistant Janitor Quitoo.

"I quit!" said Janitor Iquit.

"I quit, too!" said Assistant Janitor Quitoo.

The janitors picked up their mops and ran off

down the hall.

"This is not normal," said little Izzy Normal.

9

Ms. Cecilia Seeyalater, the school receptionist, squinted at the spill through her black-framed spectacles.

She opened the bottom drawer of her desk and took out a roll of paper towels.

"Catch!" she said as she threw the roll.

Ron Faster caught it and helped Oopsie wipe up the spill. Then, she ran back to the kindergarten room.

Ron and the other bus riders ran over to Ms. Seeyalater's desk. Beside it was a silvery stand holding a black sign with white plastic letters. The sign said,

MONDAY'S LUNCH:
BEANIE WEENIES
ON A BUN

"Hi, kids!" said Ms. Seeyalater. "Why are you late for school?"

"Mr. Stuckinaditch got stuck in a ditch," Ron told her.

"That Ivan!" said Ms. Seeyalater. "Always stuck in a ditch."

"Are we in trouble?" asked Viola Fuss.

"You're never in trouble at the Harvey N. Trouble School,"
Ms. Seeyalater said as she gave them their late passes. "Go to
class now, kids," added Ms. Seeyalater. "See you later!"

The bus kids ran up the steps to the second floor. They ran down
the hall, past the music room, where the music teacher's big orange
cat, Moose, was napping on top of the piano.
They ran to the end of the hall and into
their classroom.

A big brown briefcase was sitting
on top of Mrs. Petzgalore's desk.

A man with a pointy head was writing on the board,

Mr. Norman Don't-know,
Substitute Teacher. Thank you very much.

"Zowie!" cried Viola Fuss. "Where is our teacher? Where is Mrs. Petzgalore?"

 "I don't know," said Mr. Norman Don't-know.

"This is not normal," said little Izzy Normal.

Ron Faster sat down at his desk.

Everyone else sat down, too.

"I don't know your names," said

Mr. Norman Don't-know. "So I will call the roll." He opened the

roll book.

"Abby Birthday?" called Mr. Norman Don't-know.

 Thanks! said Abby. "How did you know it was today?"

"I don't know," said Mr. Norman Don't-know.

He called, "Anita Dawg?" **WOOF,** said Anita.

"Sid Down?" called Mr. Norman Don't-know.

 **I am sitting down,** said Sid.

Mr. Norman Don't-know peered over the roll

book. "So you are," he said.

"Ron Faster?" called Mr. Norman Don't-know.

 **HERE!** said Ron.

"Gladys Friday?" called Mr. Norman Don't-know.

 HERE! said Gladys. "And I'm glad it's Monday!"

Mr. Norman Don't-know frowned. "You mean you're Gladys Monday?" he asked.

"Yes, I am," said Gladys Friday. "And tomorrow, I'll be glad it's Tuesday."

Mr. Don't-know took a large white handkerchief out of his pocket and mopped his forehead. Then he called, "Viola Fuss?"

"I'm here," said Viola. "And I wish Mrs. Petzgalore were here, too."

"Dewey Haveto?" called Mr. Norman Don't-know.

 Do we have to answer? asked Dewey.

"I don't know," said Mr. Norman Don't-know.

Then he called, "Izzy Normal?"

"This is not normal," said little Izzy.

"Ivanna Snack?" called Mr. Norman Don't-know.

"Me, too," said Ivanna. "What have you got?"

"I don't know," said Mr. Norman Don't-know.

He called, "Adam Up?"

"Ten students plus one substitute teacher

equals eleven of us!" said Adam.

Mr. Norman Don't-know shut the roll book.

Viola Fuss raised her hand.

"Mrs. Petzgalore is teaching us about the Roman Empire," she

said. "Can you teach us about the Roman Empire, Mr. Don't-know?"

Mr. Norman Don't-know shook his pointy head. "I don't know

about the Roman Empire," he said.

"Mrs. Petzgalore is teaching us how to add fractions," said

Adam Up. "Can you teach us how to add fractions, Mr. Don't-know?"

Mr. Norman Don't-know shook his head again. "I don't know

about adding fractions," he said.

14

"Mrs. Petzgalore is teaching us that when two vowels go walking, the first does the talking," said Gladys Friday. "Can you teach us about vowels, Mr. Don't-know?"

"I don't know about vowels," said Mr. Norman Don't-know. He sighed.

"Mr. Don't-know?" said Viola Fuss. "When is Mrs. Petzgalore coming back?"

"I don't know," said Mr. Norman Don't-know.

"I hope she comes back soon!" said Dewey Haveto.

"Me, too," said Ivanna Snack.

"Me, three," said Sid Down.

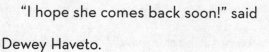

"That makes four of us," said Adam Up.

Ron Faster felt bad for Mr. Don't-know. He wanted to help him, so he said, "Mr. Don't-know? Maybe there's something inside your big brown briefcase that you could teach us about."

"I don't know," said Mr. Norman Don't-know.
Still, he popped the lock and opened his big
brown briefcase. He reached inside and pulled
out paper plates, paper cups, party hats, and
balloons. He pulled out a pitcher of fruit punch,
a tray of cupcakes with swirly pink icing, and a
plate of heart-shaped cookies with red sprinkles.

YUMMERS! cried Ivanna Snack. "What's all **THIS?**"

"I don't know," said Mr. Norman Don't-know. "I don't
know how it got into my big brown briefcase, and I don't
know how to put it back again." He scratched his pointy
head. "Maybe," he said. "Maybe . . . we should
have a birthday party for Abby Birthday."

"Do we have to?" asked Dewey Haveto.

And everybody shouted,

Then they all sang,

"Happy birthday to you!
Happy birthday to you!
Happy birthday, Abby Birthday!
Happy birthday to you!"

Mr. Norman Don't-know DID know how to blow up balloons, and for the rest of the day, the class played party games and drew on the board and ate cupcakes and heart-shaped cookies with sprinkles. The science teacher's dog, Einstein, wandered into the classroom and licked up the crumbs, and nobody said another word about Mrs. Petzgalore.

❈ ❈ ❈ ❈ ❈ ❈ ❈

After school, the bus riders got on the bus, and Mr. Ivan Stuckinaditch drove them home. When his stop came, Ron Faster jumped off the school bus and ran down the dirt road—*fast*.

He ran past the barn, where his father kept his old green race car.

He ran past the garden, where his mother grew all sorts of strange and mysterious plants.

He ran up the steps to the front porch of his big, old, full-of-junk, tumbledown house, where his parents were rocking in their rocking chairs.

"Welcome home, son," said Mr. Faster.

"I made you some rainbow-chip cookies, Ron, dear," said Mrs. Faster. She held out a platter of cookies with red, orange, yellow, green, blue, indigo, and violet chips.

Ron never ate much lunch, so he was always hungry when he got home from school. He took a warm rainbow-chip cookie and bit into it.

"Delicious, Mom," he said.

"Did you have a good day at school, son?" asked Mr. Faster.

"I had a hotsy-totsy day," said Ron.

"Tell us all about it, Ron, dear," said Mrs. Faster.

"All right," Ron said. He took another rainbow-chip cookie and told his parents all the ups and downs and ins and outs of his hotsy-totsy day.

When he had finished, Mr. Faster asked, "What did you learn at school today, son?"

Ron thought for a moment, then he said, "I learned that just because a teacher carries a big brown briefcase doesn't mean he's going to be boring."

"It's like I always say," said Mr. Faster. "You can't judge a teacher by his briefcase."

"So true," said Mrs. Faster. "And what a fine lesson that is for a hotsy-totsy Monday."

CHAPTER 2

TIPPY-TOPPY TUESDAY

On Tuesday morning, Mr. Ivan Stuckinaditch

picked up Ron Faster at the bus stop.

"Good morning, Mr. Stuckinaditch," said Ron as

he boarded the bus. Next to the driver's seat, he

spotted a gold candy box with a big red bow.

"Who's the candy for?" he asked.

"None of your beeswax," said Mr. Stuckinaditch.

Mr. Stuckinaditch picked up Viola Fuss. He picked up

little Izzy Normal. He picked up all the kids.

"Are you going to get stuck in a ditch today, Mr. Stuckinaditch?" asked Viola Fuss.

"Such a question!" said Mr. Ivan Stuckinaditch as he drove past a road crew and a sign saying,

Ivan kept driving.

The bus stopped suddenly and leaned **WAAAAAAAY** over to the left.

Ron Faster lunged—*fast*—and caught the candy box before it

hit the floor.

"**Zowie!**" cried Viola Fuss.

"**This is Not Normal,**" said little Izzy Normal.

The road crew ran over to the bus.

"Stuck in a ditch?" asked a road worker.

"That's me," said Mr. Ivan Stuckinaditch.

"Mr. Ben Diggin here," said the road worker.

"We can get you out."

Ben

Mr. Ben Diggin and his road crew lined up on the right side of

the bus and gave a mighty shove.

The bus straightened up.

Mr. Ivan Stuckinaditch hit the gas: **vrrrrm!**

The bus rolled forward, and Mr. Ivan Stuckinaditch was stuck in

a ditch no more.

The bus riders cheered, "YAY!" "YAY!" "YAY!" "YAY!" "YAY!" "YAY!"

Mr. Stuckinaditch thanked Mr. Ben Diggin and his road crew,

and then he drove the kids to school.

The kids jumped off the bus and ran into school right behind

Janitor Iquit and Assistant Janitor Quitoo, who were coming back to work.

They ran over to Ms. Seeyalater's desk. The menu sign beside it said,

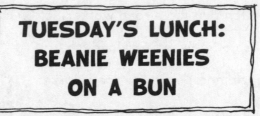

TUESDAY'S LUNCH: BEANIE WEENIES ON A BUN

Ms. Seeyalater was not sitting at her desk.

"I don't see you, Ms. Seeyalater," called Viola Fuss.

"Down here," said Ms. Seeyalater from underneath her table.

 "This is not normal," said little Izzy Normal.

"It is if you have lost your specs," said Ms. Seeyalater.

"Here they are," Ron said. He picked up her black-framed spectacles and handed them to her.

Ms. Seeyalater crawled out from under her desk and put on her specs.

26

 "I can see you now," said Ms. Seeyalater.

She squinted. "Sort of. Anyway, why are you late?"

"Mr. Stuckinaditch got stuck in a ditch," said Viola Fuss.

"That Ivan!" said Ms. Seeyalater. "Every day, stuck in a ditch!"

"Are we in trouble?" asked Viola Fuss.

"You're never in trouble at the Harvey N. Trouble School," Ms. Seeyalater said as she gave the kids their late passes.

"Go to class now, kids," said Ms. Seeyalater.

"See you later!"

They ran up the steps to their classroom.

"One step, two steps, three steps . . ." Adam Up added 'em up as they ran.

 At the top of the steps, Adam Up made an important announcement. "There are twenty-three steps," he said.

"I hope Mrs. Petzgalore is back," said Viola Fuss as they ran down the hall.

But when they got to their classroom, Mrs. Petzgalore was not there.

Mr. Norman Don't-know was not there.

A note on the board said,

> ## I am subbing for Mrs. Petzgalore today.
> ## Come down to the gym.
> ## Signed,
> ## Coach Buster Swollentoe

"This is not normal," said little Izzy Normal.

"You think Coach Swollentoe knows about the Roman Empire?" asked Viola Fuss.

"I wouldn't count on it," said Adam Up.

The kids started down the twenty-three steps. At the same time, the principal, Miss Ingashoe, started up.

They met in the middle and everybody stopped.

"Miss Ingashoe?" said Viola Fuss. "Where is Mrs. Petzgalore? Where is our teacher?"

"Mrs. Petzgalore stayed home because of a family emergency," said Miss Ingashoe. "Her dog swallowed a silver dollar."

"That's awful!" said Anita Dawg. "What did the vet say?"

 "He told her to keep an eye on the dog," said Miss Ingashoe, "and see if there's any change."

"Miss Ingashoe?" said Sid Down. "Are you still missing something?"

"Yes, I am," said Miss Ingashoe. "If you happen to find something that's missing, please bring it to the principal's office. Have a tippy-toppy Tuesday!"

Miss Ingashoe continued walking up the steps then, which was not so easy, because she was still missing something.

The kids ran down the steps, down the hallway, past the cafeteria, past the swimming pool, and to the gym. There, they found Coach Swollentoe sitting on a folding

chair. On his left foot, he wore a bright red sneaker,

but his right foot was bare. It was propped up

on his desk. His big toe looked very swollen.

"How did you hurt your toe, Coach

Swollentoe?" asked Gladys Friday.

"It's an old football injury," said Coach Swollentoe. "Acts up

now and again." He wiggled his toe.

 "Gross!" said Viola Fuss.

"All right, kids," said

Coach Swollentoe.

"Hit the floor and give me ten."

"Ten what?" said Adam Up.

"Ten push-ups," said Coach.

 "Do we have to?" asked Dewey Haveto.

"Yes, you do, Dewey," said Coach. "Do 'em nice and slow,

and I'll tell you the story of what happened to my toe."

All the kids hit the floor and began doing push-ups, nice and slow.

"One!" counted Adam Up.

"In my youth," said Coach Swollentoe, "I was the running back for the Pittstop Panthers."

"Two!" counted Adam Up.

"We were playing against the Winfield Warthogs," said Coach Swollentoe. "Biggest game of the season."

"Three!" counted Adam Up.

"The score was tied seven all," Coach went on. "There were twelve seconds left on the clock."

"Four!" counted Adam Up.

"I intercepted a pass from the Warthogs' quarterback," said Coach.

"Five!" counted Adam Up.

"I saw a hole in the defense," said Coach, "and I started running."

"Six!" counted Adam Up.

SIX!

"Coach?" said Viola Fuss. "Could you run as fast as Ron Faster?"

"I ran like the wind," said Coach Swollentoe.

SEVEN!

"Seven!" counted Adam Up.

"I zigged and I zagged," Coach Swollentoe continued. "I dodged and I darted."

EIGHT!

"Eight!" counted Adam Up.

"A pair of three-hundred-pound Warthogs waited for me at the goal line," Coach went on.

WARTHOG TOE STOMPER

NINE!

"Nine!" counted Adam Up.

"I was running for a touchdown," Coach went on, "when all of a sudden . . . good gravy!"

ANOTHER WARTHOG TOE STOMPER

Coach Swollentoe stared as the music teacher's

big orange cat raced into the gym with something

orange and hairy hanging out of its mouth.

All the kids scrambled to their feet.

"Zowie!" cried Viola Fuss. "Did Moose

catch a mouse?"

"Mice aren't orange," said Gladys Friday.

"Or hairy," said Dewey Haveto.

Just then, the music teacher,

Mrs. Doremi Fasollatido, flounced into the gym wearing a red

satin gown from her opera-singing days. She sang, "*Somebody*

catch that caaaaat! Somebody catch that caaaaaat!"

"Mrs. Fasollatido looks different today," said Ron Faster.

"Mrs. Fasollatido is bald!" cried

Abby Birthday.

"Bald as a billiard ball," said

Coach Swollentoe.

"This is Not NoRMaL," said little Izzy Normal.

The cat darted out the side door of the gym.

Mrs. Fasollatido ran up to Coach and sang,

"*I have no hair, my head is bare.*

I bought a wig for me to wear.

And with the wig, there came a cat.

And so I wear him as my hat."

SNORT!   SNORT!

Mrs. Fasollatido danced around in a circle, and continued

singing,

Thump!   Thump!

"*My kitty cat is orange and big.*

His name is Moose. He stole my wig!

Go catch him, Buster Swollentoe,

for Mrs. Fasollatido!"

"Once I could run like the wind, Doremi," said Coach

Swollentoe, "but this swollen toe has slowed me down." He turned to Ron Faster and said, "Ron, catch that cat."

"On it, Coach," said Ron.

Ron ran out the side door of the gym—

fast. He looked up and down the hallway.

No sign of the cat.

"Here, kitty!" Ron called. "Here,

Moose!"

Moose did not come.

Ron looked into Mr. Hugh da Mann's

kindergarten room.

The kindergartners were not there.

And neither was Moose.

He looked into Ms. Roxanne Pebbles's science lab.

The students were making a huge model of the moon

out of egg cartons, but Moose was nowhere to be seen.

Ron looked out a window. He saw Einstein

digging a hole next to the monkey bars,

but he did not see Moose anywhere.

He ran down the hall to the cafeteria.

There, he found a long line of kids waiting to get their beanie weenies.

Janitor Iquit and Assistant Janitor Quitoo were standing just inside the cafeteria doors. They were deep in conversation.

Mr. Hugh da Mann was leading his kindergarten class through the lunch line.

"Yer bun," said Ms. Vera Hairnet. She dropped a bun onto Chuckie Upkins's plate.

"Yer beanie weenies," said Mr. Hammond Eggz.

He slopped beanie weenies onto Chuckie Upkins's bun.

Chuckie Upkins stared at the mound of beanie weenies on his plate.

"I'm sick of beanie weenies," he said.

"Sick?" cried Mr. Hugh da Mann. He rushed over to

Chuckie. "Do you feel sick?"

"Uh-huh," said Chuckie.

"Run to the nurse's office, Chuckie!" cried Mr. Hugh da Mann. "Hurry!"

Chuckie wobbled off in the direction of the nurse's office.

Oopsie Spiller moved her tray along in the lunch line.

"Yer bun," said Ms. Vera Hairnet. She dropped a bun onto Oopsie's plate.

"Yer beanie weenies," said Mr. Hammond Eggz. He slopped beanie weenies onto Oopsie's bun.

Oopsie picked up her tray and carried it across the cafeteria. She had almost reached a table when her plate slid off her tray and crashed onto the floor.

"OOPS!" said Oopsie.

"It's all right, Oopsie!" called Mr. Hugh da Mann. "Accidents happen."

Janitor Iquit and Assistant Janitor Quitoo rushed across the cafeteria. They stared at the beanie weenies all over on the floor.

"I have an important announcement," said Janitor Iquit.

"What is it?" asked Assistant Janitor Quitoo.

"I quit!" said Janitor Iquit.

"I quit, too!" said Assistant Janitor Quitoo.

The janitors tossed their brooms over their heads and ran out of the cafeteria.

Just then, Ron spotted Moose.

The cat was peeking out from behind the trash can, eyeing the **splat** that had once been Oopsie Spiller's lunch. Moose dropped Mrs. Fasollatido's wig, dashed over to the beanie weenies, and began gobbling them up.

GOBBLE GOBBLE GOBBLE GOBBLE GOBBLE GOBBLE GOBBLE GOBBLE GOBBLE GOBBLE SNORT GOBBLE

Ron ran over and picked up Mrs. Fasollatido's wig. He waited until Moose had eaten all the beanie weenies and licked the floor. Then he snuck up on Moose from behind and

 grabbed him around the middle.

"MURP!" said Moose as Ron

picked him up.

Ron ran back to the gym—*fast*—carrying

the cat and the wig.

In the gym, Coach Swollentoe had divided all the kids into

teams. They were running relay races.

Ron spotted Mrs. Fasollatido, bald as a billiard ball, sitting in

the bleachers, looking glum.

Ron ran over to the music teacher—*fast*.

"Here is your wig, Mrs. Fasollatido," he said. "And

here is your cat."

Mrs. Fasollatido's face lit up and she burst into song.

"My kitty cat is orange and big.

His name is Moose. He stole my wig.

Ron Faster brought them back and so,

Ron Faster is my new hero!"

Mrs. Doremi Fasollatido plopped on her wig.

Moose climbed up and snuggled down on top of

Mrs. Fasollaitdo's head until it was hard to tell what

was cat and what was wig. He started purring.

Just then, the fourth-period lunch bell rang.

"Come back to the gym after you eat your beanie weenies,"

said Coach Swollentoe. "I'll set up the trampoline, and while

you're bouncing, I'll tell you what it feels like to have a three-

hundred-pound Warthog tackle stomp on your right big toe."

And that is what he did.

* * * * * * *

That afternoon, Mr. Ivan Stuckinaditch dropped Ron Faster off at the bus stop. Ron ran for home—*fast*.

He ran past the barn, where his father kept his old green race car.

He ran past the garden, where his mother grew all sorts of strange and mysterious plants.

PLEASE EXCUSE.

He ran up the front steps of his big, old, full-of-junk, tumbledown house, and into the living room, where his parents were sitting on the couch, reading.

Mr. Faster looked up from his book, *How to Get a Good Job* by

Howard I. Noh. "Welcome home, son," he said.

"Thanks, Dad," said Ron. He plopped himself down in an easy chair.

Mrs. Faster looked up from her book, *How to Look for a Job* by Dwight Way.

"Have some blueberry poppers, Ron, dear," she said.

She passed him a big bowl of what looked like bright blue popcorn.

Ron Faster took a handful.

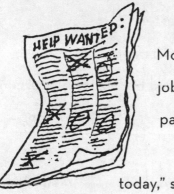

"Mmm, good, Mom," he said. "Any jobs for you in the paper?"

Mrs. Faster shook her head. "No luck today," she said.

"Any jobs for you, Dad?" asked Ron.

Mr. Faster shook his head. "Nothing for me, either," he said.

Ron took another handful of blueberry poppers and looked around the living room. Framed photographs of his father in his green race car hung all over the walls. There were newspaper

clippings, too, with bold headlines:

HUGO FASTER WINS AGAIN!
HUGO FASTER SETS NEW WORLD RECORD!
HUGO FASTER: FASTEST MAN ON EARTH!

"Why did you stop racing, Dad?" asked Ron Faster.

"I knew you would ask me that one day, son," said Mr. Faster.

"Go on and tell him, Hugo," said Mrs. Faster.

"All right, Cookie, I will,"

said Mr. Faster. He turned

to Ron.

"I drove

faster than

any other

race car

driver

in the

world," he said. "Much faster. When I raced, I won. No one could beat me. After a while, when the other drivers saw my green race car driving onto the  racetrack, they turned their cars around and drove home. The

 judge handed me the trophy and the prize money, and that was that. People stopped coming to the races." Mr. Faster shrugged. "There was only one thing for me to do, son."

"What's that, Dad?" said Ron.

"Retire," said Mr. Faster. "After I retired, the other drivers came back to the track and the races started up again."

"Do you ever think about going back to racing?" asked Ron.

"No, son," said Mr. Faster. "I'm as fast now as I ever was. If I went back to the racetrack, the same thing would happen again."

"Someday, you'll find a job you like as much as racing, Hugo," said Mrs. Faster.

"I hope so, Cookie," said Mr. Faster. "My prize money won't last forever."

Mrs. Faster popped up from the couch. "I've just had an inspiration," she said, and she ran into the kitchen.

A few minutes later, she called, "Supper's ready!"

Ron ran into the dining room—*fast*. His father was right behind him. And there, sitting on a platter in the middle of the dining table, was a model of Mr. Faster's race car made entirely from steamed green beans, except for its four potato wheels.

"Wow, Mom!" said Ron.

"My race car!" exclaimed Mr. Faster. "You're a genius, Cookie Faster!"

"Thank you, Hugo," said Mrs. Faster. She poured melted butter over the race car and served Ron the front end.

Ron took a bite of fender. "Tastes great, Mom," he said.

Mr. Faster swallowed a chunk of the left rear wheel. "Did you have a good day at school, son?" he asked.

"I had a tippy-toppy day," said Ron.

"Tell us all about it, Ron, dear," said Mrs. Faster.

"Listen to this," said Ron. Then he told his parents all the downs and ups and outs and ins of his tippy-toppy day.

"My goodness, Ron Faster!" his mother exclaimed when he'd finished. "Did you have beanie weenies on a bun for lunch?"

"No," said Ron.

Mrs. Faster smiled. "No?"

"No," said Ron. "Ms. Hairnet ran out of buns."

"Oh, dear," said Mrs. Faster.

TUESDAY'S LUNCH:
BEANIE WEENIES
~~ON A BUN~~

"What did you learn at school today, son?" asked Mr. Faster.

Ron thought for a moment, then he said, "I learned that it

doesn't matter whether you win or lose the game—it's how well you protect your toes."

"Those three-hundred-pound tackles!" Mr. Faster shook his head. "The bigger they are, the harder they stomp."

"Ouch!" said Mrs. Faster. "A heavyweight lesson for a tippy-toppy Tuesday."

CHAPTER 3

SUPER-DUPER WEDNESDAY

On Wednesday morning, Mr. Ivan Stuckinaditch picked up Ron Faster at the bus stop. He picked up Viola Fuss and little

 Izzy Normal. He picked up all the kids and headed for school.

"Don't get stuck in a ditch today, Mr. Stuckinaditch," said Viola Fuss.

"Who said that?" asked Mr. Stuckinaditch. He turned around in his seat to see—just when he should have kept his eyes on the road.

Clunk!

The front end of the bus

pitched down, and the back end

flipped up.

"Zowie!" cried Viola Fuss.

"This is not normal," said little Izzy Normal.

"Are we stuck in a ditch, Mr. Stuckinaditch?"

Ron asked.

"It's a possibility," said Mr. Stuckinaditch.

He hit the gas: **Vrrrm!**

Vrrrm!

The rear wheels spun around, but the bus stayed stuck.

"Mr. Stuckinaditch?" said Viola Fuss. "Are you going

to call Mr. Justin Case?"

"I'll think about it," said Mr. Stuckinaditch.

Mr. Stuckinaditch stood up, thinking about it. He clasped his

hands behind his back, thinking about it.

He walked toward the back of the bus, thinking about it.

When Mr. Stuckinaditch reached the back of the bus, the rear wheels hit the ground—**Thud!**—and the front wheels popped out of the ditch.

"Good thinking, Ivan!" shouted Mr. Ivan Stuckinaditch.

He raced back to the driver's seat.

But when he reached the driver's seat, the front end of the bus pitched back into the ditch  —**Clunk!**—and the rear end flipped back up.

"We're stuck in a ditch again," pointed out Viola Fuss.

"I'd better think about it some more," said Mr. Stuckinaditch.

He stood up, thinking about it.

"Wait, Mr. Stuckinaditch," called Ron Faster. "Stay where you are. Everybody else, to the back of the bus."

All the kids ran to the back of the bus. With everybody packed in the back, the rear wheels hit the ground—**Thud!**—

and the front end of the bus popped out

of the ditch.

Mr. Stuckinaditch hit the gas:

Vrrrrm! And the bus began to roll.

The bus riders cheered,

Mr. Stuckinaditch steered the rear wheels

around the ditch and drove everyone to school.

The kids jumped out of the bus and ran into

school right behind Janitor Iquit and Assistant

Janitor Quitoo, who were coming back to work.

They ran over to Ms. Seeyalater's desk. The menu beside it said,

WEDNESDAY'S LUNCH:
BEANIE WEENIES ON A BUN

Ms. Seeyalater was not sitting at her desk.

She was standing on top of it.

"This is not normal," said little

Izzy Normal.

"It is if you have just seen an enormous orange rat," said Ms. Seeyalater.

"Rats aren't orange," said Viola Fuss.

Ms. Seeyalater shivered. "I am really, really scared of rats," she said.

"Maybe you saw Mrs. Fasollatido's big orange cat," Ron said.

"Maybe I did," said Ms. Seeyalater. "That would explain why the rat was meowing."

"Maybe you need a new pair of specs," said Viola Fuss.

"Maybe I do," said Ms. Seeyalater. She jumped down from her desk. "I will call Dr. Kent Seewell and have my eyes checked. Now, why are you late?"

"Mr. Stuckinaditch got stuck in a ditch," Ron told her.

"That Ivan!" Ms. Seeyalater said. "Maybe he should get *his* eyes checked."

"Are we in trouble?" asked Viola Fuss.

"You're never in trouble at the Harvey N. Trouble School," Ms. Seeyalater said as she gave out late passes.

"Go to class now, kids," added Ms. Seeyalater. "See you later!"

Everyone raced for the steps as Mrs. Doremi Fasollatido, bald as a billiard ball, flounced across the reception area in a blue velvet gown from her opera-singing days. She was singing,

"My Moosie cat has run away!
He stole my wig again today!
Do I know why he does it? No!
Poor Mrs. Fasollatido!"

At that moment, the principal, Miss Ingashoe, walked into school, which was not so easy because she was missing something. In her right hand, she held an orange wig.

"Are you missing something, Mrs. Fasollatido?" she asked.

"Oh, my goodness, yes! How ever did you guess?" sang Mrs. Fasollatido.

Miss Ingashoe gave Mrs. Fasollatido her wig.

"Thank you, Miss Ingashoe! I'm so grateful to you!" she sang as she put it on.

"You're welcome," said Miss Ingashoe. "Now, only one of us is missing something."

All the kids ran up to the principal.

"Miss Ingashoe?" said Viola Fuss. "Is Mrs. Petzgalore here today?"

"No, she had to stay home because of a family emergency," said Miss Ingashoe. "Her bunny rabbit swallowed a spoon."

"That's awful!" said Anita Dawg. "What did the vet say?"

"He told her to keep the bunny quiet and make sure it doesn't stir," said Miss Ingashoe. "Have a super-duper day!" She walked off then, which was not so easy because she was the one

still missing something.

As the kids started up the

stairs, Gladys Friday stopped.

"P.U.," she said. "Something

smells."

"I don't smell anything," said Chuckie Upkins, coming

out from behind the stairs and wobbling off

in the direction of the nurse's office.

The kids ran to the top of the twenty-

three steps, and to their classroom. When they got there, they

found another note on the board:

> **Mrs. Petzgalore is still out,**
> **so you will spend the day with me.**
> **Come down to the science lab right away.**
> **We'll have a blast!**
> **Ms. Roxanne Pebbles**

"**This is not normal,**" said little Izzy Normal.

"Science?" said Viola Fuss. "Now, we'll never learn
about the Roman Empire!"

Everyone ran back down the twenty-three steps.

They ran past Mr. Hugh da Mann's kindergarten classroom.
Ron Faster looked in and saw that it was Oopsie Spiller's
turn for show-and-tell.

"It took my brother a year to put together this jigsaw puzzle and—
OOPS!" said Oopsie.

The kids ran into the science lab, where they found Ms. Roxanne

Pebbles wearing an orange jumpsuit and a pair of protective goggles.

"Good morning, future scientists!" she said.

In one corner of the lab sat the huge model of the moon

made out of egg cartons. The counters were lined with sprouting

potatoes, green and purple molds, test tubes filled with powders and liquids, and all sorts of weird-looking science projects.

Ms. Pebbles's dog, Einstein, was guarding the door to the lab.

"May I pet Einstein, Ms. Pebbles?" asked Anita Dawg. "Please! Please!"

"Canines enjoy a good rub on the abdomen," said Ms. Pebbles. "Go to it."

Anita Dawg ran over to Einstein.

"Einey-steiney," she crooned as she scratched him behind the ears.

Einstein smiled. He didn't open his eyes, but he rolled over so that Anita Dawg could rub his abdomen.

"Sit down, future scientists," said Ms. Pebbles.

"I am sitting down," said Sid Down.

"Here's a scientific question for you," said Ms. Pebbles. "What is a volcano?"

No one raised a hand.

"A volcano is a mountain with a really

bad temper!" said Ms. Pebbles.

She cracked up, laughing.

"Here's another one," said Ms. Pebbles. "What

did the scientist say when the volcano erupted?"

No hands went up.

"IT'S A LAVA-LY DAY!" shouted Ms. Pebbles.

She laughed so hard at that one, she had to take off her protective

goggles and wipe her eyes. When she finally stopped laughing,

she put her goggles back on and said, "Who knows what we call

scientists who study volcanoes?"

 Not even Viola Fuss raised her hand.

"Volcanologists," said Ms. Pebbles. "Today, you are

going to be volcanologists and make a model of a volcano."

"Do we have to?" asked Dewey Haveto.

"Yes, we do, Dewey," said Ms. Pebbles. "And we are

going to make that volcano erupt—**BOOM!**"

"YAY!" "YAY!" "YAY!" "YA "YAY!" "YAY!" everybody cheered.

Ms. Pebbles picked up the trash can. "Ron Faster, run outside and fill this up with dirt and rocks and pebbles." She handed Ron the trash can and a shovel.

"On it," Ron said.

"Einstein will help you," Ms. Pebbles said. "Einstein? Go dig!"

At the sound of the word "dig," Einstein's small, black eyes popped open. His pointy ears stood straight up. He sprang to his feet, gave himself a shake, and raced out of the science lab.

"Dog gone!" said Anita Dawg.

Ron Faster ran after Einstein—*fast*. They ran down the hall and into the reception area.

Ms. Seeyalater squinted at Einstein racing toward her.

"I hope that's not a rat!" she cried.

"It's not!" called Ron Faster.

At that moment, Luke Out, the kindergarten door monitor, opened the door, and Mr. Hugh da Mann began leading his kindergarten class in from the playground.

"Look at the doggie!" said Chuckie Upkins.

"Nice doggie!" said Iona Tricycle.

Einstein barreled toward the kindergartners.

"*LOOK OUT!*" shouted Mr. Hugh da Mann.

"What did I do?" said Luke Out.

The kindergartners scattered in all directions, yelling and shrieking.

Luke Out, the kindergarten door monitor, froze.

Einstein zoomed out the door. Ron raced out behind him.

Einstein ran to a spot at the far end of the playground. Ron ran after him.

Einstein started digging. Ron shoveled the dirt and rocks and pebbles that he dug up into the trash can. Pretty soon, the trash can was full.

"Stop digging, Einstein," said Ron.

Einstein kept on digging.

"Einstein, stop!" said Ron.

But Einstein did not stop, so Ron ran

back into school and through the reception area—*fast*—carrying a trash can full of dirt and rocks and pebbles.

He ran past the
cafeteria line, which was
so long, it snaked all

the way past the science lab. Ron squeezed by, and

when he reached the lab, he put the trash can

down in front of Ms. Pebbles.

"Einstein is still outside, digging," he told her.

"Oh, he buried a bone out there," said Ms. Pebbles. "He must be

digging it up." She put a big square of plywood down on the floor

and passed out supplies. "All right, volcanologists," she said. "You

know what to do."

Anita Dawg and little Izzy Normal knelt down and

glued an empty dog-food can to the center of the plywood. Ivanna

Snack and Adam Up put one end of a wrapping-

paper tube into the can and held it there while Sid Down and

Gladys Friday mixed the dirt and rocks and pebbles with enough

water to make them stick together.

Abby Birthday and Dewey Haveto patted the wet dirt and rocks and pebbles around the wrapping-paper tube. When they got tired of patting, Viola Fuss and Ron Faster took over. Soon, the volcano was finished.

"Good work, volcanologists," said Ms. Pebbles. "Get ready to have a blast! Where are my volunteers?"

Holding test tubes filled with liquids, Adam Up, Viola Fuss, Sid Down, and Abby Birthday came up to the volcano. Anita Dawg came, too, holding a tablespoon and a box of baking soda.

"Water," said Adam. He emptied his test tube into the mouth of the volcano.

"Dish soap," said Gladys. She emptied her test tube into the mouth of the volcano.

"Red food color," said Sid. He emptied his test tube into the mouth of the volcano.

"Vinegar," said Abby. She emptied her test tube into the mouth of the volcano.

red food coloring

vinegar

water

dish soap

"Baking soda," said Anita.

She was about to scoop a tablespoon of baking soda from the box, when Ms. Roxanne Pebbles held up a hand and said, "Stop!"

Anita stopped.

"Vinegar is an acid," said Ms. Roxanne Pebbles. "Baking soda is a base. What happens when you mix an acid with a base?"

Everybody yelled, "BOOM!"

"Exactly!" said Ms. Pebbles.

Just then, Einstein burst into the science lab carrying something in his mouth.

"Einey-steiney!" cried Anita Dawg. She dropped the box of baking soda into the mouth of the volcano, and ran over to the dog. "Did you dig up your bone?"

"That doesn't look like a bone," said Sid Down.

"It looks like a shoe," said Ron Faster.

"It's Miss Ingashoe's shoe!" cried Viola Fuss.

Ms. Pebbles gasped. "So that's what Einstein buried out there."

Ms. Pebbles crouched down low and began walking toward her dog.

"Come here, Einstein," she said. "Let me have that shoe."

When she got close, Einstein darted away.

"Come here, Einey-steiney," said Anita Dawg. She grabbed for the shoe, but Einstein jerked his head away and ran.

"Einstein, sit!" said Sid Down.

Einstein did not sit.

Soon, everybody was chasing Einstein around the science lab.

 "This is not normal," said little Izzy Normal.

"Hey!" said Adam Up. "When ten students plus one science teacher are chasing a dog, what time is it?"

"I don't know," said Abby Birthday.

"Eleven after one!" said Adam Up.

Ron joined the chase. He zigged and he zagged and

he quickly backed Einstein into a corner. Everybody

crouched down and inched toward the dog, blocking

his escape.

Einstein dangled the shoe by

its heel, and smiled.

"You think it's a game, don't you, Einey-steiney?" said Anita

Dawg.

Viola Fuss wrinkled her nose.

"Something smells," she said.

Ron sniffed. He smelled

something, too. And it wasn't

Chuckie Upkins.

"Look!" cried Gladys Friday.

"The volcano!"

Everybody turned to look.

Red foam was bubbling out of the volcano, and suddenly—

BOOM!

Dirt and rocks and pebbles flew in all directions.

"Thomas Alva Edison!" exclaimed Ms. Pebbles.

Einstein dropped the shoe, yelped, and tore out of the science lab.

"Volcanologists! Hit the floor and cover your heads!"

cried Ms. Pebbles as dirt and rocks and pebbles showered down

from the ceiling.

Everybody hit the floor.

"This is not normal!" cried little Izzy Normal.

At last, the dirt and rocks and pebbles stopped falling, and everybody got up.

"Is everybody okey-dokey?" asked Ms. Roxanne Pebbles.

Everybody was.

Ms. Pebbles picked up the shoe. It was smashed and dirty, and covered with tooth marks.

"I'd better fix this up before I give it back to Miss Ingashoe," she said. Then she turned to Ron. "Ron Faster, please run and get the janitors."

"On it," Ron said, and off he ran—*fast.*

He ran back with Janitor Iquit and Assistant Janitor Quitoo.

The janitors stopped in the doorway. They stared at the dirt and rocks and pebbles all over the floor, all over the desks, all over the huge model of the moon made of egg cartons, and all over all the science projects.

"I have an important announcement," said Janitor Iquit.

"What is it?" said Ms. Roxanne Pebbles.

"I quit!" said Janitor Iquit.

"I quit, too!" said Assistant Janitor Quitoo.

The janitors kicked up their heels and ran off down the hall.

"This is not normal," said little Izzy Normal.

"We had a blast, didn't we, volcanologists?" said Ms. Pebbles.

Everybody yelled, **"YES!"**

"Now, who can tell me what we call scientists who study dirt and rocks and pebbles?" asked Ms. Pebbles.

No hands went up.

"Geologists," said Ms. Pebbles. "Geologists, please take out your notebooks and pencils."

Ron opened his backpack to take out his notebook. Inside, he found a box with a red bow.

A note attached to the bow said,

Oodles of
poodles. Enjoy!
Love, Mom

"Zowie!" said Viola Fuss. "Open it!"

Ron untied the bow, opened the sack, and pulled out a yellow

cracker shaped exactly like a French poodle.

"Cheese Poodles!" said Ron, and he passed the bag around.

There were enough so that everyone got three, including

Ms. Roxanne Pebbles.

"Crunchy on the outside," said Ivanna Snack.

"Chewey on the inside," said Dewey Haveto.

 "Delish," said Anita Dawg, and she wolfed down all three.

When all the Cheese Poodles were gone, Ms. Pebbles handed out magnifying glasses and microscopes and for the rest of the afternoon, the geologists studied dirt and rocks and pebbles.

✿ ✿ ✿ ✿ ✿ ✿ ✿

When Ron Faster jumped off the school bus that afternoon, he ran for home—*fast*.

He ran past the barn, where his father kept his old green race car.

 He ran past the garden, where his mother grew all sorts of strange and mysterious plants.

BURP!

He ran up the steps of his big, old, full-of-junk, tumbledown house and into the kitchen.

"Welcome home, son," said his father, who was sitting at the kitchen table chopping red and green and purple tomatoes.

"Hello, Ron, dear," said his mother, who stood at the kitchen table kneading dough—*fast*. "What's the best thing about eating pizza?"

"Biting the point off a slice," said Ron.

"Precisely," said Mrs. Faster. She flipped the dough into the air, where it expanded into the shape of a star, and caught it on a pizza tray. "This pizza is going to have plenty of points."

Mr. Faster lined up tomatoes on top of the dough in red, green, and purple stripes.

Mrs. Faster grated on cheese—lots and lots of cheese—and popped the pizza into the oven.

While his parents were busy with the pizza, Ron sat down at the kitchen table and looked around the room. The walls were covered with framed photographs of his mother wearing a tall chef's hat and standing beside important-looking people. There were newspaper clippings, too, with bold headlines:

MAYOR CLAIMS COOKIE FASTER BAKES WORLD'S BEST COOKIES!

GOVERNOR HIRES TOP CHEF COOKIE FASTER AWAY FROM MAYOR!

SENATOR GAINS FORTY POUNDS; BLAMES CHEF COOKIE FASTER!

"Mom?" said Ron. "Why did you stop being a chef?"

"I knew you would ask me that one day, Ron, dear," said Mrs. Faster.

"Go ahead and tell him, Cookie," said Mr. Faster.

"All right, Hugo, I will," said Mrs. Faster. She turned to Ron. "Before you were born, Ron, dear," she said, "I was chef for lots of bigwigs. They all loved my cooking. But in the end, they all said, 'Cookie Faster, you're fired.'"

"Why, Mom?" asked Ron.

Mrs. Faster shrugged.

"I'd go into the kitchen," she said, "and in no time at all, I might whip up my Jack-Be-Little Pumpkin Soup, my Emerald City Salad,

my Six Drumsticks Roasted Chicken, my Carrot Chorus, my Broccoli Bouquet, and my Three Cheers Chocolate Cake, and nobody but nobody could eat fast enough to keep up with me."

"Couldn't you slow down, Mom?" asked Ron.

"Can you run slowly, Ron Faster?" asked his mother.

"Impossible," said Ron Faster.

"And I can't cook slowly," said Mrs. Faster. "When you're a Faster, you're faster, and that's all there is to it."

"Someday you'll find the perfect cooking job, Cookie," said Mr. Faster.

"I hope so, Hugo," said Mrs. Faster. "My severance pay won't last forever."

Mrs. Faster's timer dinged. She took the star-shaped red-green-and-purple-striped pizza out of the oven, sliced it into lots of star-shaped pieces, and passed it around.

Ron took a hot slice and bit off a purple point. Then he bit off two red points. And then two green ones. "This is the best

pizza ever, Mom," he said.

"Did you have a good day at school, son?" asked Mr. Faster.

"I had a super-duper day," said Ron. "And everybody loved your Cheese Poodles, Mom."

Cookie Faster smiled. "Please tell us all about your day, Ron, dear," she said as she poured three tall glasses of pink watermelonade.

"Here goes," said Ron. He told his parents all about the ups and outs and downs and ins of his super-duper day.

"This was the most exciting day all week, Ron Faster!" exclaimed Mrs. Faster.

"What did you learn in school today, son?" asked Mr. Faster.

Ron thought for a moment, then he said, "I learned that just because a dog is digging, doesn't mean he's digging for a bone."

"Assume nothing!" shouted Mr. Faster. "And don't count your

bones before they're dug up."

Mrs. Faster winked at Ron and said, "A very deep lesson for a super-duper Wednesday."

CHAPTER 4

HUNKY-DORY THURSDAY

On Thursday morning, Mr. Ivan Stuckinaditch picked Ron up at the bus stop.

"Good morning, Mr. Stuckinaditch," said Ron as he boarded the bus.

"If you say so," said Mr. Stuckinaditch.

Mr. Ivan Stuckinaditch picked up Viola Fuss.

 He picked up little Izzy Normal. He picked up all the kids and headed for school.

"See any ditches in the road today, Mr. Stuckinaditch?" asked Viola Fuss.

Mr. Stuckinaditch narrowed his eyes and stared at the road. "All clear ahead!" he said.

Just then, Ron Faster spotted an enormous ditch in the road.

"Look out for the ditch, Mr. Stuckinaditch!" he shouted.

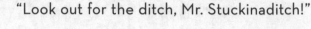

"I see it!" said Mr. Stuckinaditch. He swerved to miss it, and flipped the bus upside down.

"Zowie!" cried Viola Fuss.

"This is not normal!" said little Izzy Normal.

"Is everybody okey-dokey?" asked Mr. Stuckinaditch.

Everybody was.

Just then, a large red truck drove up the road. The truck stopped. The driver stuck his head out the window.

"You flip the bus?" he said.

"No, the name's Stuckinaditch," said Mr. Stuckinaditch.
"Ivan Stuckinaditch."

"Preston de Gass, here," said the truck driver. "I can help you."

Mr. Preston de Gass flipped a switch inside the cab of his truck and pressed on the gas. A crane popped up. A cable dangled down from it with a big hook at the end.

Mr. Preston de Gass jumped out of his truck and attached the hook to the rear bumper of the school bus.

"Hold on tight!" he called, and he jumped back into his truck.

Mr. Stuckinaditch and all the kids held on tight as Mr. Preston de Gass pressed on the gas and the crane pulled the school bus into the air, with the rear bumper up, and the front bumper down.

"Zowie!" said Viola Fuss.

"This is not normal!" said little Izzy Normal.

"Wheeeee!" said Mr. Stuckinaditch.

Ron Faster and all the kids held on tight as Mr. Preston de Gass lowered the bus. He gently set down the front wheels, and when he touched the back wheels to the ground, the bus was right-side up again.

The bus riders cheered,

"YAY!" "YAY!" "YAY!" "YAY!" "YAY!" "YAY!"

Mr. Preston de Gass jumped out of his truck and unhooked the hook from the bumper of the bus. He jumped back into his truck and pressed on the gas and lowered his crane. Mr. Stuckinaditch thanked Mr. Preston de Gass. Then, Mr. Preston de Gass pressed on the gas and drove away, and Mr. Stuckinaditch drove everyone to school.

The kids jumped off the bus and ran into school right behind Janitor Iquit and Assistant Janitor Quitoo, who were coming back to work. They ran over to Ms. Seeyalater's desk.

The menu beside it said,

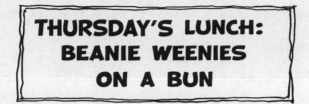

THURSDAY'S LUNCH:
BEANIE WEENIES
ON A BUN

Ms. Seeyalater was sitting at her desk wearing a pair of

sparkly new specs.

"I like your fancy new glasses, Ms. Seeyalater," said Viola

Fuss.

"I can *really* see you now," said Ms. Seeyalater. "Dr. Kent Seewell fixed me right up. Let me guess why you're late. Ivan got stuck in a ditch."

"No," said Ron Faster. "Mr. Stuckinaditch flipped the bus upside down."

"I must speak to Ivan!" said Ms. Seeyalater.

"Are we in trouble?" asked Viola Fuss.

"You're never in trouble at the Harvey N. Trouble School," Ms. Seeyalater said as she gave everyone a late pass.

"Go to class now, kids," said Ms. Seeyalater. "See you later!"

The kids raced toward the steps. They reached them just as Miss Ingashoe was walking down, which was not so easy because she was missing something.

"Miss Ingashoe?" said Viola Fuss. "Did Mrs. Petzgalore come to school today?"

Miss Ingashoe shook her head. "Mrs. Petzgalore had to stay home because of a family emergency," she said. "Her monkey swallowed her ballpoint pen."

"**Oh, no!**" cried Anita Dawg. "What did the vet say?"

"He told Mrs. Petzgalore to use a pencil," said Miss Ingashoe.

"Miss Ingashoe?" said Sid Down. "Are you still missing something?"

"Yes, I am," said Miss Ingashoe. "Have a hunky-dory Thursday!"

Miss Ingashoe continued down the twenty-three steps, which was not so easy because she was still missing something. The kids ran up the steps and down the hall to their classroom.

When they got there, they found another note on the board:

> **THE K-KIDS ARE WAITING FOR**
> **THEIR BUDDIES IN THE KINDERGARTEN**
> **ROOM. COME ON DOWN!**
> **SIGNED,**
>
> **MR. HUGH da MANN**

"This is not normal," said little Izzy Normal.

"Do you think they study the Roman Empire in kindergarten?" said Viola Fuss.

"I don't think so," said Ivanna Snack. "But they have snacktime!"

Ron Faster led the way back down the twenty-three steps, down the hall, and to the kindergarten room. He opened the door a crack and everyone peeked in. The kindergartners were having show-and-tell.

"This is my pet, Cutie Pie," Iona Tricycle was saying. She held up a white rat with pink eyes and a long pink tail.

"Thank you, Iona," said

Mr. Hugh da Mann, who had on a blue shirt and a red tie.

"Please put Cutie Pie back in his cage. And now, K-kids, look

who's here."

"**OUR BUDDIES!**" shrieked the kindergartners.

"Come in, buddies," said Mr. Hugh da Mann. "What do we say

to our buddies, K-kids?"

"**WELCOME, BUDDIES!**" shouted the kindergartners.

"Good job, K-kids," said Mr. Hugh da Mann. "Now, hold up your buddy signs."

The kindergartners held up signs on which they

had printed names.

Luke Out held up a sign that said **VIOLA**.

Viola Fuss ran over to him. "Hi, buddy!" she said.

Iona Tricycle held up a sign that said **ADAM**.

Adam Up ran over to her. "How many

wheels on a tricycle?" he asked her.

"You want to pet Cutie Pie?" asked Iona.

Oopsie Spiller held up a sign that said **IZZY**.

Little Izzy Normal ran over to her. "This is not

normal," he said.

Chuckie Upkins held up a sign that said **RON**.

Ron ran over to him—*fast*. "Hi, Chuckie,"

he said. "I'm your buddy, Ron Faster."

"Hi, buddy," said Chuckie.

When everyone had a buddy, Mr. da Mann said, "Everybody sit

down."

"I am sitting down," said Sid Down.

"We are lucky to have our buddies with us today, aren't we,

K-kids?" said Mr. Hugh da Mann.

 **"YES, MR. DA MANN!"** shouted the

kindergartners.

"K-kids," said Mr. da Mann, "do you think our

buddies would like to help us make goodies for

our bake sale tomorrow?"

"Yes, Mr. da Mann!" shouted

Ivanna Snack.

"First, we will make Kindergarten Krunch Balls," said

Mr. Hugh da Mann.

All the kids washed their hands while Mr. Hugh da Mann

covered the tables with brown paper and put out small containers

of oats, dried cranberries, raisins, and brown sugar.

Ron Faster sat down beside Chuckie. He took some oats and cranberries and raisins and sticky brown sugar and rolled them together into a ball.

"One Kindergarten Krunch Ball," said Ron. "Your turn, Chuckie."

Chuckie took oats and cranberries and raisins and brown

sugar and rolled them into a ball. Ron and Chuckie kept rolling. Pretty soon, they'd made ten Kindergarten Krunch Balls.

"Let's wrap them up for the bake sale," Ron said. He ran over to Mr. Hugh da Mann's desk to get some plastic wrap. When he got back, there were only three Kindergarten Krunch Balls on the table.

"What happened to the other Krunch Balls, Chuckie?" Ron asked.

"I don't feel so good," said Chuckie.

Mr. Hugh da Mann ran over to the table. "Chuckie, do you feel sick?" he asked.

"Uh-huh." Chuckie nodded.

"Quick! Go to the nurse's office," said

Nurse's Office →

Mr. Hugh da Mann. "Your buddy will go with you."

"Let's go, Chuckie!" said Ron.

Ron took Chuckie's sticky hand and the two of them walked out of the kindergarten room.

Chuckie walked slowly. Very slowly.

"How do you feel, Chuckie?" Ron asked.

"Uнннн," groaned Chuckie.

"Can you go any faster?" Ron asked.

"Noooo," said Chuckie.

"Are you going to make it to the nurse's office?" Ron asked.

"I never do," said Chuckie.

"I have an idea," Ron said. He grabbed Chuckie around the middle and picked him up.

"**BURP!**" said Chuckie, and Ron took off running—*fast.*

Ms. Seeyalater looked through her sparkly new specs and saw Ron carrying Chuckie in the direction of the nurse's office.

"Run faster, Ron Faster!" she called.

Ron Faster ran faster.

"Uhhhh," groaned Chuckie. His tummy gurgled.

"Hold on!" Ron told him. "We're almost there!"

Ron rounded a corner and ran down the hall to the nurse's office.

The school nurse, Mr. Arthur Mometer, was sitting at his desk.

"May I help you?" he asked as Ron ran past him with Chuckie and into the bathroom.

"We made it!" Ron said as he put Chuckie down.

And in the nick of time, too.

When Chuckie came out of the bathroom, Mr. Mometer said, "Congratulations, Chuckie! You made it to the nurse's office!"

Chuckie grinned.

"Let's get our thermometer," said Mr. Arthur Mometer, "and check your temperature." He poked a thermometer into Chuckie's mouth.

After a minute, Mr. Arthur Mometer took out the thermometer.

"Normal," he said. "You may go back to class."

Ron and Chuckie headed back to the kindergarten room, but when they got there, it was empty.

"Everyone must be at lunch," Ron said. "Let's go."

They walked down the hall, past a long line of kids waiting to get their beanie weenies.

Janitor Iquit and Assistant Janitor Quitoo were standing inside the cafeteria doors. They were deep in conversation.

Ron and Chuckie lined up behind Mr. Hugh da Mann and the rest of the K-kids, and finally it was their turn to get lunch.

"Yer bun," said Ms. Vera Hairnet. She dropped a bun onto Chuckie's plate.

"Yer beanie weenies," said Mr. Hammond Eggz. He was about to slop the beanie weenies onto Chuckie's bun when Chuckie said, "STOP!"

Mr. Eggz stopped.

"We have beanie weenies every day," said Chuckie Upkins.

"That's right," said Mr. Eggz.

"Beanie weenies make me sick!" said Chuckie Upkins.

"Me, too!" called someone from the back of the line.

"Me, too!" called someone else.

Voices rang out all over the cafeteria:

"Me, too!"

"Me, too!"

"Me, too!"

When the voices stopped, Adam Up called, "That makes fifty-six of us!"

"I have an important announcement!" said Mr. Hammond Eggz.

"What is it?" asked Ms. Vera Hairnet.

"I quit!" said Mr. Hammond Eggz.

"I quit, too!" said Ms. Vera Hairnet.

The cafeteria workers untied their aprons and threw them on the floor.

"Way to go!" called Janitor Iquit from the doorway.

"Aw, right!" called Assistant Janitor Quitoo.

The janitors clapped and whistled as Mr. Hammond Eggz and Ms. Vera Hairnet stomped out of the cafeteria. Mr. Eggz and Ms. Hairnet stomped right by Miss Ingashoe, who had arrived late to the scene because she was missing something. They kept on stomping, right out of school.

"K-kids and buddies," said Mr. Hugh da Mann,

"follow me back to the kindergarten room. We will have double snacktime today."

"**YAY!**" shouted Ivanna Snack.

Ron's class walked back down the hall with their kindergarten buddies.

They passed Mrs. Doremi Fasollatido walking up the hall, wearing a silvery gown from her opera-singing days. Moose was curled up on top of her orange wig, purring loudly.

They walked past the gym, where Coach Swollentoe sat on a folding chair, his right foot propped up on his desk.

They walked past the swimming pool. Ron looked in through the glass square on the door and saw Ms. Roxanne Pebbles. She was calling Einstein, who was splashing around in the water. Ms. Pebbles looked as if she could use some help.

"Be right back, Chuckie," Ron said to his buddy. He swung open the door and ran to the swimming pool—*fast*.

"Ms. Pebbles!" Ron said. "What's Einstein doing in the pool?"

"The dog paddle!" said Ms. Pebbles, and she cracked up laughing at her own joke. When she finally stopped laughing, she said, "Can you help me get him out of there?"

"On it," Ron said.

Ron knew that Einstein loved two things: digging and shoes.

"Einstein!" Ron called as he whipped off his left sneaker. "Fetch!"

He threw his shoe onto the edge of the pool beside the shallow-end steps.

Einstein's small, black eyes lit up when he spotted the shoe. He dog-paddled over to the steps and leaped out of the pool. As he sank his teeth into the sneaker, Ron snuck up on him from behind and grabbed him around the middle.

"**WURP!**" said Einstein as Ron picked him up.

Ron handed the wet dog to Ms. Pebbles, and she snapped on his leash.

"Good work, Ron Faster," said Ms. Pebbles. "Thank you."

"You're welcome," Ron said. Then he ran to the kindergarten room—*fast*—just in time for a **DOUBLE** SNACK.

After snacktime, Mr. Hugh da Mann said, "K-kids and buddies, now it's time to make brownies and peanut brittle for our bake sale tomorrow."

"Do we have to?" asked Dewey Haveto.

"Yes, we do, Dewey!" said Ivanna Snack.

"We will cook in the school kitchen," said Mr. Hugh da Mann.

He passed out ingredients and cooking tools for everyone to carry.

He gave Chuckie Upkins a bag of flour.

He gave Iona Tricycle a bag of sugar.

He gave Oopsie Spiller a wooden spoon.

"Can I carry the eggs,

Mr. da Mann?" said Oopsie. "Please! Please let me!"

"Will you be extra careful with them, Oopsie?" asked

Mr. da Mann.

"Yes!" said Oopsie. "I promise!"

Mr. Hugh da Mann handed her a large plastic bowl filled with eggs.

The K-kids lined up. They walked out of their classroom and through the reception area.

Ms. Seeyalater looked at the K-kids and their buddies through her sparkly new specs.

"Where are you going?" she asked.

"To the school kitchen," said Luke Out.

"Our class is making brownies for our bake sa—**OOPS!**" said Oopsie as the bowl slipped out of her hands. Eggs flew out of the bowl and hit the floor, splattering all over the place.

"It's okay, Oopsie," said Mr. Hugh da Mann. "Accidents happen."

Ms. Seeyalater punched Janitor Iquit's number into her phone.

Janitor Iquit and Assistant Janitor Quitoo rushed to the scene.

The janitors looked at the splattered eggs.

"Ms. Seeyalater," said Janitor Iquit, "I have an important announcement."

"What is it?" said Ms. Seeyalater.

"I quit!" said Janitor Iquit, tossing his broom over his head.

"I quit, too!" said Assistant Janitor Quitoo, tossing his broom, too.

The janitors leaped over the broken eggs and ran out of school.

Ms. Seeyalater opened her middle desk drawer and took out a gold candy box with a big red bow.

"You kids clean up those eggs," she said, "and there's

chocolate in your future."

"We can do it in two minutes!"
said Adam Up. He picked up a mop.

Ivanna Snack picked up another.

Ms. Seeyalater tossed Ron a roll of paper towels.

Two minutes later, the floor was
shining and all the kids were chewing on chocolates.

"Thanks for spilling, Oopsie," said Ivanna Snack.

"Anytime," said Oopsie.

"Can I have another piece?" asked Chuckie.

"One to a customer," said Ms. Seeyalater.

"Ms. Seeyalater?" said Viola Fuss.
"Who gave you the box of chocolates?"

"Somebody wonderful," said
Ms. Seeyalater. And her face
turned as red as the bow on
the box of chocolates.

When everyone had finished their
chocolates, Mr. Hugh da Mann said, "I have an
important announcement."

"What is it?" asked Oopsie Spiller.

"I am going to make brownies and peanut
brittle at home tonight," said Mr. da Mann.
"Right now, line up! We're going out to the playground for
double recess."

All the kids cheered, "YAY!" "YAY!" "YAY!" "YAY!" "YAY!" "YAY!"

Out on the playground, Ron showed Chuckie
how to run—*fast*.

"Thanks, buddy," said Chuckie. "Now
I can make it to the nurse's
office every time!"

After that, Ron and his
friends and the K-kids

jumped rope . . .

and played kickball . . .

and freeze tag . . .

until it was time to go to home.

* * * * * * *

Half an hour later, Ron Faster jumped off the school bus and

ran for home—*fast.*

He ran past the barn, where his father was

tuning up his old green race car.

"Hi, Dad!" Ron called as he ran past.

Mr. Faster waved. "Welcome home, son!"

he called.

Ron Faster ran past the garden, where his mother was

pulling weeds.

"Hi, Mom!"

called Ron.

"Come over to the

garden, Ron,

dear!"

called his

mother.

Ron ran over—*fast*.

Mr. Faster ran over, too—even *faster*.

"How come you're working on your race car, Dad?" asked Ron, as he sat down on a garden bench.

"I'm going to drive your mother somewhere tomorrow, son," said Mr. Faster.

Mrs. Faster handed Ron a basket of warm Pirate Muffins for his after-school snack.

"Mmmmm," said Ron, which was about all anyone could say with a mouth full of Pirate Muffin, filled with chocolate chips and cherry bits, and other yummy buried treasures.

Mr. and Mrs. Faster sat down on the garden bench across from Ron and helped themselves to Pirate Muffins, too.

"Did you have a good day at school, son?" asked Mr. Faster.

"I had a hunky-dory day," said Ron.

"Please tell us all about it," said his mother.

"Here's what happened," said Ron. Then he told his parents all the ins and ups and outs and downs of his hunky-dory day.

"Amazing, Ron Faster!" said Mrs. Faster. "Was there anything inside your piece of chocolate candy?"

"Caramel," said Ron.

"Mmmm," said Mrs. Faster.

"What did you learn at school today, son?" asked Mr. Faster.

"That's easy," said Ron. "I learned that if fifty-six kids get together, it's bye-bye, beanie weenies."

"Things happen when you stick together," Mr. Faster declared. "There's strength in numbers!"

"Speaking of numbers," said Mrs. Faster, "that makes two reasons that today is a hunky-dory Thursday."

"Two?" said Ron. "You mean beanies and weenies?"

"No," said Mrs. Faster. "I mean no more beanie

weenies *and* I got a phone call this afternoon about a job."

"Congratulations, Mom!" said Ron. "Are you going to be a chef again?"

"Yes, I am," said Mrs. Faster. "I'll find out all about the job tomorrow morning when your father drives me to work."

"Ah-ha!" said Ron. "So that's why you were tuning up your race car, Dad."

"That's right," said Mr. Faster. Then he shook his head and said, "But it won't be easy."

"What, driving Mom to work?" asked Ron.

"No," said Mr. Faster. "Sticking to the speed limit."

CHAPTER 5

YOWIE-KA-ZOWIE FRIDAY

On Friday morning, Mr. Faster drove his

green race car out of the barn—*fast.* He squealed to

a stop in front of the big, old, full-of-junk, tumbledown house and

tooted the horn.

Mrs. Faster and Ron ran out of the house and jumped into the

race car. Mr. Faster drove up the road with his family squished

together inside the race car like canned

sardines.

At the school bus stop, Ron jumped
out of the race car.

"Have a good day at school,
Ron, dear," said Mrs. Faster.

"Good luck with the job, Mom!" said Ron. He waved as his
father drove down the road—not *too* fast.

Soon, a big yellow bus pulled up.

"All aboard!" said Mr. Ivan Stuckinaditch, who was wearing a
pair of yellow-framed specs that matched the bus.

"I like your

new glasses,
Mr. Stuckinaditch,"
said Ron as he boarded the bus.

"Thank you," said Mr. Ivan
Stuckinaditch. "Dr. Kent Seewell fixed me right up."

Mr. Stuckinaditch picked up Viola Fuss.

 He picked up little Izzy Normal.

He picked up all the

kids and headed for school.

"Are you going to get stuck in a ditch today, Mr. Stuckinaditch?"

asked Ron.

"Why all the fuss about ditches?" muttered Mr. Stuckinaditch.

"Are you talking to me?" asked Viola Fuss.

"I am not," said Mr. Stuckinaditch.

"Mr. Stuckinaditch?" said Ivanna

Snack. "How come you've got a bouquet

of roses next to your driver's seat?"

"None of your beeswax," said Mr. Ivan Stuckinaditch. Then, he

looked at the road through his new yellow

 specs and drove the bus all the

way to school without getting

stuck in a ditch, not even once.

As he jumped off the bus, Ron spotted a green race car in the school parking lot. It had black-and-white racing stripes on the front hood, just like his father's green race car. And there was his father, walking toward the bus.

"Hello, son," said Mr. Faster.

"Hi, Dad," said Ron. "What are you doing here?"

"Just stopped by to say hello," said Mr. Faster.

Everyone from the bus gathered around Ron and his dad, including Ivan Stuckinaditch.

"Are you really Hugo Faster, the famous race car driver?" asked Mr. Stuckinaditch.

"Yes, I am," said Mr. Faster. "Are you really Mr. Ivan Stuckinaditch, the famous school bus driver?"

"Yes, I am," said Mr. Ivan Stuckinaditch. "I used to be Isadore Stuckinaditch," he added, "but I changed my name."

Mr. Faster patted the hood of the bus. "How fast does this baby go?" he asked.

"On a straight road with no ditches?" said Mr. Stuckinaditch. "I can get her up to forty-five."

Mr. Faster nodded.

"How about your race car?" asked Mr. Stuckinaditch. "I'll bet you can really let 'er rip."

"Oh, sure." Mr. Faster

nodded. "Stuckinaditch," he added, "do you know what the most

dangerous part of a race car is?"

Mr. Stuckinaditch frowned. "I don't believe I do," he said.

"It's the nut behind the wheel," said Mr. Faster.

"Har-har!" laughed Mr. Stuckinaditch. "That's a good one,

Faster!"

"Mr. Faster?" said Viola Fuss. "May I have your

autograph?"

Mr. Faster signed Viola's notebook.

"See you, Dad," said Ron, and he ran into

school with his friends, right behind Janitor Iquit

and Assistant Janitor Quitoo, who were

coming back to work.

All the kids ran over to the

receptionist's desk, where Iona Tricycle was showing

Cutie Pie to Ms. Seeyalater.

"He's so soft!" Ms. Seeyalater was saying as she

held Cutie Pie and stroked his fur.

"And what a darling pink nose!"

She turned to the bus riders.

"Hi, kids!" she said. "Have

you seen Iona's guinea pig?"

"Cutie Pie isn't a guinea

pig, Ms. Seeyalater," said

Iona Tricycle.

"He isn't?" said Ms. Seeyalater.

"No," said Iona. "Cutie Pie is

a rat."

"He IS?" Ms. Seeyalater

stared at Cutie Pie through her sparkly new specs. "This is the

first time I've seen a rat up close," she said. "He really is a little

cutie pie." And she handed Cutie Pie back to Iona.

Viola Fuss saw the menu first. She shouted,

"Yowie-ka-zowie!"

FRIDAY'S LUNCH:
CARTWHEEL SOUP
HEADSTAND SANDWICHES
SOMERSAULT CHIPS
BACKBEND COOKIES

Ron stared at the menu. His mother sometimes made him Cartwheel Soup. He looked up, and there was his mother walking toward him wearing a tall white chef's hat.

"Hello, Ron, dear," said Mrs. Faster.

"Mom!" exclaimed Ron. "This is your new job?"

Mrs. Faster nodded. "I wanted to surprise you." She smiled.

"Miss Ingashoe called me yesterday afternoon and told me she was missing something."

"Miss Ingashoe called to tell you she was missing her shoe?" asked Ron.

"No," said Mrs. Faster. "She called to tell me she was missing her cafeteria workers. She said she'd heard that Cookie Faster cooked fast, and never, ever made beanie weenies. When I told her both were true, she hired me."

FRIDAY'S LUNCH:
CARTWHEEL SOUP
HEADSTAND SANDWICHES
SOMERSAULT CHIPS
BACKBEND COOKIES

"Are you really Cookie Faster, the famous chef?" asked Viola Fuss.

"Yes, I am," said Mrs. Faster.

"May I have your autograph?" asked Viola.

Mrs. Faster signed Viola's notebook and then she said, "I'd better get back to the kitchen. See you at lunch, Ron, dear!"

"See you, Mom," said Ron.

"So, kids," asked Ms. Seeyalater, "why are you late today?"

"We're not late, Ms. Seeyalater," said Ron Faster. "We're right on time."

Ms. Seeyalater looked at her watch through her sparkly new specs. "So you are," she said. "How did *that* happen?"

"Mr. Stuckinaditch did not get stuck in a ditch today," said Viola Fuss.

"And that is not normal," said little Izzy Normal.

"It is if Dr. Kent Seewell fixed him right up with a new pair of specs," said Ms. Seeyalater, looking particularly pleased.

"We know who gave you that box of chocolates," said Viola Fuss.

"Go to class now, kids," said Ms. Seeyalater.

But they did not go because just then, Mr. Ivan Stuckinaditch and Mr. Hugo Faster walked into the reception area. Mr. Stuckinaditch was holding the bouquet of roses behind his back.

"Ivan!" said Ms. Seeyalater. "I like your new yellow specs."

"Dr. Kent Seewell fixed me right up," said Mr. Stuckinaditch. "I like your new specs, too, Cecilia."

"Thank you," said Ms. Seeyalater.

"Thank YOU," said Mr. Stuckinaditch. He whisked the roses out from behind his back and handed them to Ms. Seeyalater. "Will you marry me, Cecilia?"

"Oh, Ivan!" cried Ms. Seeyalater, and her face turned as red as the roses. "Of course I will!"

"Yowie-ka-zowie!" said Viola Fuss.

Everybody cheered,

"YAY!" "YAY!" "YAY!" "YAY!" "YAY!" "YAY!" "YAY!"

When the cheering died down, Mr. Stuckinaditch said, "While we're away on our honeymoon, Hugo Faster is going to drive the school bus."

All the bus riders cheered, "YAY!" "YAY!" "YAY!" "YAY!" "YA" "YAY!"

"Ivan and I are going to take 'er out for a test run now," said Mr. Faster.

"See you later, Cecilia Seeyalater," said Mr. Stuckinaditch.

He and Mr. Faster left the building.

"Ms. Seeyalater?" said Viola Fuss. "Are you going to change your name to Cecilia Stuckinaditch?"

"Beautiful," murmured Ms. Seeyalater, who had not quite

recovered from Ivan's proposal. "See you later, kids!"

Everybody ran for the steps.

But no one ran up, because at the foot of the steps, Mr. Hugh da Mann and his kindergarten class had set up their bake sale. Coach Swollentoe, wearing both his bright red sneakers again, was sampling the peanut brittle. Ms. Pebbles was buying Kindergarten Krunch Balls. Einstein was under the table licking up crumbs.

All the kids crowded around the bake sale.

"Kindergarten Krunch Balls!" called Chuckie Upkins. "One to a customer!"

"I'll take one Kindergarten Krunch Ball, two peanut brittle packets, and three brownies," said Adam Up. "Add 'em up."

The school principal, Miss Ingashoe, walked over to the bake sale, which was not so easy because she was missing something.

"Oh, Miss Ingashoe," said Ms. Roxanne Pebbles. "I believe I have what you've been missing." She reached into her bag and pulled out a shoe, which was no longer smashed or dirty or tooth-marked.

Miss Ingashoe took the shoe and put it on. It matched her other shoe perfectly.

"If the shoe fits, wear it," she said, smiling. "Thank you,

Ms. Pebbles. Wherever did you find what was missing?"

"I didn't find it," said Ms. Pebbles. "Einstein did."

(She did not say a word about how Einstein had stolen the shoe in the first place, chewed on it, buried it, and dug it up again.)

The principal patted Einstein on the head. "Good boy!" she said.

Einstein gave Miss Ingashoe's shoe one last lick.

Just then, Oopsie Spiller picked up a big silver platter of brownies.

"Who would like to buy some of Mr. Hugh

da Mann's delicious brownies?" she called.

"Let me help you with that, Oopsie," said Mr. da Mann. He whisked the platter from her and walked out from behind the bake sale table when, without warning, the silver platter somersaulted out of his hands and crashed to the floor. Brownies flew in all directions.

"OOPS!" said Mr. Hugh da Mann.

"It's okay, Mr. da Mann," said Oopsie. "Accidents happen."

Janitor Iquit and Assistant Janitor Quitoo heard the crash, picked up their brooms, and came dashing to the scene.

The janitors looked at the brownies scattered all over the place.

"I have an important announcement," said Janitor Iquit.

But before Janitor Iquit could say, "I quit!" and before Assistant Janitor Quitoo could say, "I quit, too," who

should come walking down the steps wearing a golden gown and golden slippers from her opera-singing days, but Mrs. Doremi Fasollatido? Halfway down the stairs, she stopped. She stared at the brownies all over the floor. Moose poked his head up and stared at the brownies, too.

Mrs. Fasollatido sang,

"Dear janitors, there's been a spill!

Quick! Sweep it up! Please say you will!

Please do not quit! Please do not go!

Sings Mrs. Fasollaitdo."

"Brava, Doremi!" the janitors shouted.

"Brava!"

"Sing to us, Doremi!" cried Janitor Iquit. "And we'll never quit again!"

"Never!" cried Assistant Janitor Quitoo. "Ever!"

"If you will stay, I'll sing all day!"

sang Doremi Fasollatido. And she

burst into song:

"Dear janitors, you sweep and mop,
you clean the school, please never stop!
And now we'd like to thank you two,
so listen while we sing to you!"

Mrs. Fasollatido waved her arms, beckoning everyone to join

her in singing.

"Do we have to sing?" asked Dewey Haveto.

"Yes, *you* do, Dewey!" sang Mrs. Fasollatido.

"To the tune of 'Happy Birthday!' Everybody sing!"

And everybody sang,

> *"Thank you, Janitor Iquit!*
>
> *Thank you, Janitor Quitoo!*
>
> *Never quit again, dear janitors.*
>
> *We'll always need you."*

Then Janitor Iquit and Assistant Janitor Quitoo

kicked up their heels and began to sweep up the

brownies. And as they swept, they sang in

deep, booming baritone voices,

"La la la broom-dee-yay!

La la la broom-dee-yay!

You la la spill the beans,

the la la floor we cleans.

The la la juice you slop,

we la la get the mop.

La la volcano BOOM!

we la la get the broom.

La la the eggs go CRACK!

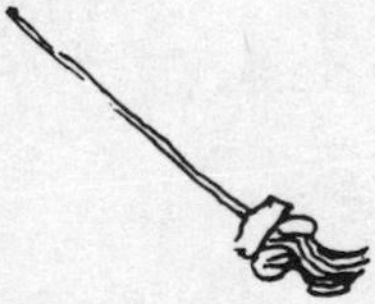

we la la mop attack.

La la la uppy chuck,

we la la mop it up.

You la la keep it up,

we la la sweep it up.

La la la broom-dee-yay!

La la la BROOM!"

"Bravo, janitors!" cried Mrs. Doremi Fasollatido. "What

voices! We must sing together!" She turned around and hurried up

the stairs, beckoning the janitors to follow her to the music room.

When Mrs. Fasollatido and the janitors

had disappeared, Ron Faster and all the kids

in his class raced up the steps.

"I'm glad it's Friday!" shouted Gladys Friday as

they ran down the hallway and into their classroom.

And there, standing beside the teacher's desk,

was their very own teacher.

"Yowie-ka-zowie!" said Viola Fuss.

"Mrs. Petzgalore!" cried Ron Faster.

"You're back!"

"That's right," said Mrs. Petzgalore, who was wearing a floor-length white robe. Gold bracelets circled her

arms. A large owl was perched on her shoulder. He blinked sleepily as the students came into the classroom.

"How is your dog?" asked Anita Dawg.

"Fine," said Mrs. Petzgalore.

 "How is your bunny rabbit?" asked Dewey Haveto.

"Dandy," said Mrs. Petzgalore.

"How is your monkey?" asked Sid Down.

"Up to his old tricks," said Mrs. Petzgalore. "Take your seats, senators."

Everyone sat down, even Sid Down.

"Who can tell me," said Mrs. Petzgalore, "which goddess from ancient Roman mythology sprang fully grown from Jupiter's head and kept an owl as her companion?"

"Minerva!" shouted Viola Fuss. "Goddess of wisdom!"

"**THIS** is normal!" shouted little Izzy Normal.

Ron Faster could hear the sweet, high notes of Mrs. Doremi Fasollatido's voice and the deep, booming voices of the janitors echoing from down the hallway. He smiled. Friday had hardly begun, and already it had been totally **yowie-ka-zowie**.

❄ ❄ ❄ ❄ ❄ ❄ ❄

After school, Mr. Ivan Stuckinaditch hummed happily to himself as he drove the kids home. When his turn came, Ron Faster jumped off the school bus, and there was his father sitting in the driver's seat of his green sports car, waiting for him at the bus stop.

"Hop in, son," he said. "I drove your mother home from school. I thought maybe you could use a lift today, too."

"Thanks, Dad," said Ron. He climbed into the passenger seat and fastened his seat belt.

Mr. Faster stepped on the gas. He left a cloud of dust behind as he drove down the dirt road. Ron looked out the window as they whizzed past the barn, home to the green race car, and

past the garden, where his mother grew all sorts of strange and mysterious plants.

Mr. Faster squealed to a stop in front of their big, old, full-of-junk, tumbledown house, and there was Mrs. Faster, sitting in a rocking chair on the front porch.

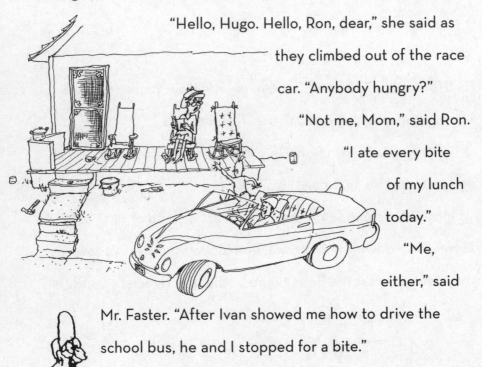

"Hello, Hugo. Hello, Ron, dear," she said as they climbed out of the race car. "Anybody hungry?"

"Not me, Mom," said Ron. "I ate every bite of my lunch today."

"Me, either," said Mr. Faster. "After Ivan showed me how to drive the school bus, he and I stopped for a bite."

"Let's just sit then," said Cookie Faster.

Mr. Faster sat down in a rocker and Ron sat down in another rocker, and the Faster family rocked—*fast*.

"Did you have a good first day on the job, Mom?" asked Ron.

"Yes, I did, Ron, dear," said Mrs. Faster. "I cooked as fast as I could, and it was exactly fast enough. I believe I have found my dream job." She looked thoughtful. "I wonder what I'll cook for lunch on Monday."

"Did you have a good day, Dad?" asked Ron.

"I had an excellent day, son," said Mr. Faster. "I got the race car tuned up, I

learned how to drive a school bus, and I didn't get a single traffic ticket."

"What about you, Ron, dear?" said Mrs. Faster. "Did you have a good day at school?"

"I had a **yowie-ka-zowie day**," said Ron. "Mrs. Petzgalore came back and all the kids loved your lunch."

"It's been quite a week, hasn't it?" asked Mr. Faster. "What have you learned at school, son?"

Ron thought for a moment. His head was stuffed with so many things he had learned this week, it was hard to pick just one.

"I learned," he said at last, "that there's no place on earth like my **hotsy-totsy, tippy-toppy, super-duper, hunky-dory, yowie-ka-zowie SCHOOL**."

"You can say that again, son," said Mr. Faster.

"There's no place on earth like my **hotsy-totsy, tippy-toppy, super-duper, hunky-dory, yowie-ka-zowie SCHOOL**," said Ron.

"That's my boy!" said Mr. Faster.

Mrs. Faster smiled. "You're a spoke off the old wheel, Ron, dear," she said.

The Fasters talked on and on until it was nearly dark. Mrs. Faster ran into the kitchen and whipped up a Very Veggie Pie with a Mashed Potato Crust. Mr. Faster brought out little tables, and they ate outside on

the porch, sitting in their rockers. When they finished eating, Cookie Faster popped up again.

"Looks like your mother's off her rocker, son," said Mr. Faster.

"Ha-ha, Dad," said Ron.

Cookie Faster came back outside carrying a platter.

"Night Sky Treats!" she announced. "I've got marshmallow moons covered with powdered-sugar space dust, cotton candy comets with orange caramel tails, and twinkling peppermint stars."

Ron chose a cotton candy comet and bit off the tail.

"Cosmic, Mom," he said.

Mr. Faster picked up a marshmallow moon and took a bite.

"Mmmm," he said. "You are out of this world, Cookie Faster."

Mrs. Faster helped herself to a pair of peppermint stars.

"I can almost taste the space dust," she said.

Ron Faster and Hugo Faster and Cookie Faster ate their Night Sky Treats as they watched the moon rise and the stars come out. They stayed out on the porch and rocked until the whole sky lit up. Then, they went inside their big, old, full-of-junk, tumbledown house, and went to bed.

THE END

ABOUT THE AUTHOR

KATE McMULLAN taught sixth grade in Compton, California. She had one toad, two snakes, two guinea pigs, and thirty-two future scientists in her class. Her students once designed an experiment to see whether tomato plants grew better if they were exposed to no music, classical music, or rock music. (Rock music won!) Another time, they built a volcano that erupted, sending out so much smoke that the entire school had to be evacuated. (Everyone was okey-dokey.) Kate has written more than one hundred books for children. Yes, Adam Up, that's one hundred books! Visit her on the Web at katemcmullan.com.

ABOUT THE ILLUSTRATOR

While serving in the Marines, **GEORGE BOOTH** got his start in cartooning by working as a cartoonist for *Leatherneck* magazine. His illustrations have since appeared in *The New Yorker*, *The New York Times*, and several children's books. His newest book, *Starlight Goes to Town*, written by Harry Allard, was published in Fall 2008 by FSG. George and his wife, Dione, live in Stony Brook, New York.

GOFISH

QUESTIONS FOR THE AUTHOR

KATE MCMULLAN

When did you realize you wanted to be a writer?
When I read *The Secrets of Good Writing* by Kent Tellu.

What's your most embarrassing childhood memory?
The day I accidentally threw my retainer into the trash at lunch. I had to go back to the cafeteria and dig through the garbage until I found it. My friend Luke Harder came with me, and he was a big help.

What's your favorite childhood memory?
Riding the school bus with Ivan Stuckinaditch's cousin, Ron Offderode.

As a young person, who did you look up to most?
The tallest kid in the class, of course, who was Stella Growin.

What was your favorite thing about school?
Math class! (That's what my friend Eliza Lot told me to say.)

What was your least favorite thing about school?
Running races at recess. My friend Denise Hoyt felt the same way.

What did you want to be when you grew up?
A race car driver, just like Mr. Hugo Faster.

Were you a reader or a non-reader growing up?
Definitely a reader! My favorite books were *Shocking Stories* by Alec Tricity and *Running to the Outhouse* by Will E. Makeit.

What book is on your nightstand now?
Have a Hot Time! by Hal A. Penno.

What inspired you to write *School!*?
The great cartoonist George Booth (no joke!) and, as always, my muses, Toby and Pinkie.

Muses: Toby and Pinkie

What sparked your imagination for *School!*?
Bad knock-knock jokes! Here's the worst one I know.
  Knock, knock!
  Who's there?
  Lois.
  Lois who?
  Lois the dachshund to the ground.
(I told you it was bad!)

Which of your characters is most like you?
Ivanna Snack. My friend Eaton D. Cheeze and I are always hungry.

What's your favorite TV show or movie?
I like TV medical dramas, and my friend Sarah Doctorindy-
haus does, too.

Do you ever get writers' block?
Not personally, but my friend Kent Dewitt has a terrible time
with writers' block. Maybe he needs a more positive attitude.

**What do you want readers to remember about your
books?**
To buy the next one, like my friend Rita Book.

**What would your readers be most surprised to learn
about you?**
I am a serious person, just like my friend Hewlett D. Dawg-
saut. Very serious.

GOFISH

QUESTIONS FOR THE AUTHOR

GEORGE BOOTH

What did you want to be when you grew up?
A cartoonist. I started drawing when I was three. My mother saw possibilities, so she provided plenty of paper and pencils.

When did you realize you wanted to be an illustrator?
When I worked in Washington DC, in an office with an excellent illustrator, Sergeant John DeGrasse. He insisted a cartoonist had to have a broad definition. I researched in the library, created a reference morgue, and attended life and painting classes at the Corcoran School of Art at night.

How did you celebrate publishing your first book?
I smiled. It was a Dr. Seuss book, *Wacky Wednesday*.

Where do you work on your illustrations?
At my drawing board in my studio.

If you were a character from *School!*, who would you be?
Ivan Stuckinaditch.

Where do you go for peace and quiet?
I get in bed with my pussycat, Puddin'.

What makes you laugh out loud?
My daughter, Sarah.

Who is your favorite fictional character?
SpongeBob.

If you were stranded on a desert island, who would you want for company?
President Obama!

Who is your favorite artist?
Dr. Seuss!

GAMES INSPIRED BY
SCHOOL!
ADVENTURES AT THE
HARVEY N. TROUBLE
ELEMENTARY SCHOOL

① **Match the trick words on the left to the real location on the right.**

1.	Army Knee Ah	Greece
2.	Bar Bade Ohs	Botswana
3.	Boo Tan	Chile
4.	Bowl Livia	Haiti
5.	Boats Wanna	Seychelles
6.	Bueno Sigh Rays	Nepal
7.	Chilly	Pakistan
8.	Ya Booty	Armenia
9.	Grease	Philippines
10.	Hate He	Bhutan
11.	Nay Paul	Bolivia
12.	Pack His Tan	Djibouti
13.	Phillip Pees	Barbados
14.	Say Shells	Buenos Aires

 Which school supplies are being disguised by these puns?

1. eRazor   ....

2. Pent Sill   ....

3. Chock Bored   ....

4. Hi Lie Tear   ....

5. Pay Per   ....

6. Why Tout   ....

7. Cal Cool Later   ....

③ Think of the word that SOUNDS like the first but is spelled differently.

1. What we throw in the trash is WASTE, but a belt goes around our ....

2. When we make a mistake, we ERR, but when we breathe, we inhale ....

3. A plant that grows by a river is a REED, but when we look at books, we ....

4. For homework you use a pencil to WRITE, and when you get the answers

   correct, you know you were ....

5. When you blink or look at things you use your EYE, but when you talk about

   yourself, you call yourself ....

6. To make a desk you need a wooden BOARD, but when you're not interested,

   you're most likely ....

7. If you're going too fast on your bike, you must use the BRAKE, but if you crash,

   your bike might ....

8. When you walk into a store, you see what they have to SELL, but a microscopic

   part of your body is a ....

9. A train you didn't catch was MISSED, but another word for fog is ....

④ Circle the correct word for what is shown in the picture.

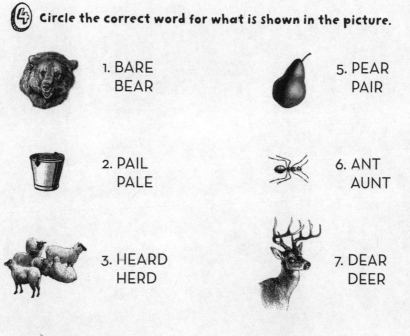

1. BARE
   BEAR

2. PAIL
   PALE

3. HEARD
   HERD

4. BURY
   BERRY

5. PEAR
   PAIR

6. ANT
   AUNT

7. DEAR
   DEER

8. TOW
   TOE

ANSWER KEYS

Answer Key (1)

1. Armenia
2. Barbados
3. Bhutan
4. Bolivia
5. Botswana
6. Buenos Aires
7. Chile
8. Djibouti
9. Greece
10. Haiti
11. Nepal
12. Pakistan
13. Philippines
14. Seychelles

Answer Key (2)

1. eraser
2. pencil
3. chalkboard
4. highlighter
5. paper
6. Wite-Out
7. calculator

Answer Key (3)

1. waist
2. air
3. read
4. right
5. I
6. bored
7. break
8. cell
9. mist

Answer Key (4)

1. BEAR
2. PAIL
3. HERD
4. BERRY
5. PEAR
6. ANT
7. DEER
8. TOE